Clean-up Day

Story by Kathryn Sutherland
Illustrations by Virginia Gray

Contents

Chapter 1

A Note in the Mailbox

Tilly found a note in the mailbox.
She took it inside and gave it to her mother.

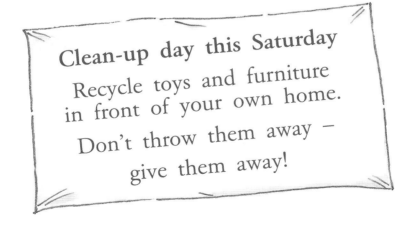

Clean-up day this Saturday
Recycle toys and furniture
in front of your own home.
Don't throw them away —
give them away!

"That's a good idea," said Mum.
"We should recycle more."

"We already recycle cans, bottles and paper," said Tilly.

"But we could all do more," said Mum. "The rubbish tip is filled with more than rubbish. People throw away things others could use."

"I have plenty of toys I don't use," said Tilly. "Other kids could have them."

"Yes," Mum agreed. "You could give them away instead of leaving them all over your room."

Tilly's bedroom was a mess. Mum spoke sternly to her.
"I can't believe this mess!" she said.
"There are clothes in your bookcase
and at least twenty toys on the floor.
Please clean up your room."

"That will take the whole day!" groaned Tilly.

"Perhaps, but it's a good chance to search
for toys to recycle," Mum said.

Chapter 2

Cleaning Up

Tilly didn't like cleaning up. But she enjoyed it more when she put on her favourite music.
She danced as she picked things up off the floor.

Mum brought in a large box.
"Gather the toys you're recycling," she said,
"and put them in here for Saturday."

Tilly found it hard to decide which things to keep and which to give away, but slowly the box filled and the floor emptied.

Later, Mum said, "Great work, Tilly. I'm amazed. Your room looks so different.
It's ages since we've seen your floor!"

Chapter 3

Recycling Day

On Saturday morning, Tilly placed the toys
on a rug near the edge of the grass.
Mum and Dad brought out a colourful bookcase,
Tilly's old high chair and some kitchen things.

Soon a family stopped to look at the high chair.

"Take it for your baby. I'm much too big for it now," Tilly laughed.

"It's just right. Thank you," said the man.

"Would your baby like my old giraffe, too?"
asked Tilly.

"Yes," said the baby's mother.
"He'll enjoy playing with that."

Two sisters from across the road
took the bookcase.

"We need a bookcase," said one of them.

"Although the colours don't match our living room,
it's a good size," said the other.

"You could paint it," said Tilly. "Take it.
We bought a bigger bookcase
because we have so many books."

"Thanks very much," they said.

Chapter 4

Hassan's Toys

Later, Tilly's friend Hassan, from next door, came out carrying a large box.

"Hi, Hassan. Are you recycling some toys, too?" asked Tilly.

"Yes," he replied. "Come and look."

Tilly went over. "Are you really giving away your skates?" she asked.

"They're too small for me now.
Have them if they fit," said Hassan.

"Are you sure?" said Tilly. "Thanks.
They're the right size."

Tilly kept looking.
"Are you throwing out your spaceman?" she asked.

"Yes, I hardly ever play with him," replied Hassan.
"Take him."

"Great," said Tilly, then, "Oh, I love this game!"

"Take it. I don't need it," said Hassan.

"Thanks. I'll get my box to put these things in,"
said Tilly.

Tilly's box was soon full of Hassan's toys and games.
She felt a little bit uncertain
about the amount she had in the box
and asked, "Have I taken too much?"

"No," Hassan replied. "I'm happy for you to have them."

"Thanks," said Tilly.
"Come over and play with them any time."

That evening, most things Tilly's family had left out
for recycling had gone.

"There's hardly anything to bring back inside," Tilly said.

"Nothing except a few toys and cups," said Dad.
"I'll give those to the second-hand shop.
Then everything will be recycled."

Next morning, Tilly said,
"I wonder if that baby is sitting
in my old high chair eating breakfast."

"He's probably making a mess, like you did,"
Mum replied.

"Was I messy?" asked Tilly.

"Yes, you were!" laughed Dad. "You're the same now!"

"Except your room isn't messy
now you've given away so much," said Mum.

Tilly pulled a funny face.

"It's not messy again, is it?" asked Mum.

Mum and Dad stood at Tilly's door
with their mouths open.

"Hassan said I could have these," grinned Tilly.
"Recycling's great. When's the next clean-up day?"